I0451194

Stolen

PRAISE FOR *STORYSHARES*

"One of the brightest innovators and game-changers in the education industry."
– Forbes

"Your success in applying research-validated practices to promote literacy serves as a valuable model for other organizations seeking to create evidence-based literacy programs."

- Library of Congress

"We need powerful social and educational innovation, and Storyshares is breaking new ground. The organization addresses critical problems facing our students and teachers. I am excited about the strategies it brings to the collective work of making sure every student has an equal chance in life."
– Teach For America

"Around the world, this is one of the up-and-coming trailblazers changing the landscape of literacy and education."
- International Literacy Association

"It's the perfect idea. There's really nothing like this. I mean wow, this will be a wonderful experience for young people."   - Andrea Davis Pinkney, Executive Director, Scholastic

"Reading for meaning opens opportunities for a lifetime of learning. Providing emerging readers with engaging texts that are designed to offer both challenges and support for each individual will improve their lives for years to come. Storyshares is a wonderful start."
- David Rose, Co-founder of CAST & UDL

Stolen

Robert Wonders

STORYSHARES

Story Share, Inc.
New York. Boston. Philadelphia

Copyright © 2022 by Robert Wonders

All rights reserved.

Published in the United States by Story Share, Inc.

The characters and events in this book are fictitious. Any similarity to real persons, living or dead, is entirely coincidental.

Storyshares
Story Share, Inc.
24 N. Bryn Mawr Avenue #340
Bryn Mawr, PA 19010-3304
www.storyshares.org

Inspiring reading with a new kind of book.

Interest Level: Middle School
Grade Level Equivalent: 4.0

9781642615395

Book design by Storyshares

Printed in the United States of America

Storyshares Presents

1

Finally, the final fifth grade bell rang. Annie Kellogg and Aariz Ishmael hurried out the doors of the Eastside Elementary School. They started walking down Elm Street to the Goodman Public Library. Today they had volunteered to help at the library bake sale. It was one of several fundraisers for library renovation.

"How much money do you think they'll make this week?" asked Annie.

"Lots if I get to eat what I want," laughed Aariz.

"You're always hungry," said Annie. "Well, you'd better hurry. Today's the last day of the sale."

"Do you think they'll replace the entire bank part?" asked Aariz. Half of the library was converted from the town's old bank. "I really like all the weathered wooden beams and old brickwork from the 1800s."

"I heard that they're going to replace only part of the building. I think they want to keep all that history."

"I hope I have time to browse the new mystery books," said Aariz. "I wonder if *Hidden Staircase* is out yet."

Annie turned to Aariz and grinned. "Beat you to it. I reserved the last copy online yesterday."

Aariz snickered. "Figures. Well, read it fast, then let me borrow it before it's due. That way I'll get it faster and you'll avoid your usual late fee. For now I'll reread the Sherlock Holmes mysteries instead. There's nothing like classic whodunits."

They walked into the library and were cheerfully greeted by Cathy Roberts, one of the assistant librarians. She sat behind the main desk, organizing returned books.

"You two are just in time. We can use help to display all these great looking baked goods," Miss Roberts said.

She led the children to the community room. On the way, they passed old Mrs. Harrison, the head librarian, who mumbled a greeting as she shuffled a book cart toward the back of the library.

"Not the friendliest person," said Annie with a frown.

Aariz just shrugged. He was eyeing the delicious baked goods on the tables ahead.

Mr. Lasker, the custodian, had worked at the library for as long as anyone could remember. He was setting up a table.

"Hello, you two," he said with a tired smile. "Aariz, can you give me a hand with this last table?"

Aariz eagerly ran over to help. He liked Mr. Lasker, who often showed him around the old bank part of the library and told Aariz about its fascinating history. Some of the old file drawers and deposit boxes were still there.

People came to the bake sale throughout the rest of day. Aariz was so busy that he could only sigh as items that he wanted were quickly bought. He did manage to buy a package of cookies just before the sale ended though.

After the sale, Miss Roberts stood at the front desk and counted the money.

"Looks like this was a big success. We've raised over $1,200 to help expand the library. I'd better put this away in the safe for now."

As the library was closing, Annie and Aariz went back out into the warm autumn air. Aariz handed Annie one of his cookies as they walked back to their homes.

2

When Annie and Aariz arrived at the library three days later, they saw three police cars in the parking lot.

"I wonder what's going on?" asked Aariz.

Inside, Mrs. Harrison was speaking to a police officer. Annie and Aariz walked over to Miss Roberts at the checkout counter.

"Why are the police here, Miss Roberts?" asked Annie.

Miss Roberts forced a weak smile. "The evening of the bake sale, Mrs. Harrison discovered that the bake sale money was missing. I had to stay after the library closed on another matter and she left after me, as she often does.

"The next morning, the police came to search the library. They left with an old bank deposit box from the basement. This isn't the first time money has gone missing from the library. A month ago, we had another library fundraiser by the Soccer Club. Afterward, we found that some of that money was missing. The police searched the entire library but had no luck. It's still under investigation. And now this."

Just then a detective appeared from around a corner. Annie overheard him speaking to Mrs. Harrison.

"Who besides you had the combination to the safe in your office?" asked the detective.

"Just me and Ed Lasker. We had problems with the safe locking properly. He has locksmithing experience and fixed it, so he knew the combination. You don't think..."

"What about Miss Roberts?" continued the detective. "Didn't she place the money in the safe?"

"Yes. I saw her go to the safe with the money, but I already had it open on another matter. She doesn't have the combination."

The detective nodded and paused before continuing. "The day after the robbery we found some of the stolen money in an old bank deposit box in the basement. We took it to the station, checked it for fingerprints, and found the custodian's prints on it. We have every library employee's fingerprints on file from the Soccer Club robbery. No other prints were on it."

A few minutes later an officer appeared with Mr. Lasker in handcuffs.

Mr. Lasker was shaking his head. His eyes were wide and pleading. "I didn't take the money," he said to the detective. "I handled a lot of those old bank boxes. A lot of them were for a historical exhibit for Miss Roberts. I don't know anything about the missing money."

"Looks like we got a break," said the detective to Mrs. Harrison. He turned to Mr. Lasker. "You can tell us all about it down at the station." He motioned to the officer to take him away.

Annie and Aariz couldn't believe it. They had known Mr. Lasker for years. He was always helpful. He often bought them donuts from the coffee shop.

"Aariz, we need to talk about this," said Annie.

"Then let's go talk about this at the coffee shop and get something to eat. I'm starving!"

"You're always starving. Are you buying?"

Aariz's stomach won out. "Yeah, I'm buying. But nothing expensive."

They sat at a table in the coffee shop, each with a bagel and apple juice.

"I think Mrs. Harrison has something to do with it," said Annie. "She's mean to everyone. And she was the one who discovered the money was missing. And she also stayed late that night."

"But she reported the robbery," said Aariz.

"That was to deflect suspicion away from her," said Annie. "I think we should investigate."

"I think we should let the police investigate," argued Aariz. He knew that Annie's love of mysteries often led to trouble— mostly his trouble.

"Mrs. Harrison and Mr. Lasker were the only people who had the combination to the safe," said Annie. "Mr. Lasker couldn't have done it. I'm sure of it. Mrs. Harrison knew he handled those deposit boxes. Maybe she hid some of the money there on purpose so the police would find it."

Aariz thought a moment. "That's possible. I also don't believe that Mr. Lasker stole the money. But we need evidence."

"Let's hide in the library tonight," said Annie. "Maybe we can find something. Mr. Lasker needs help, and that help is us."

"What about our parents?"

Annie thought for a moment. "If they ask, I'm at your house doing homework and you're at my house doing homework. We both get great grades. We do homework together all the time."

Aariz looked up toward the ceiling, silently pleading for someone to talk him out of this.

Stolen

3

That night, they hid in the library computer room until everyone left. It was dark and eerie, not at all the warm, familiar place it usually was. After fifteen minutes, Annie motioned to Aariz. They slowly tiptoed out of the computer room and over to the library bookshelves. They went quietly from shelf to shelf, carefully looking around as they went.

Suddenly, Annie jumped and almost screamed when they heard a sharp crack. Aariz turned to Annie and put his finger to his lips.

"It's just the wind blowing a tree branch against the building," he whispered.

Aariz turned back around and froze. Ahead of them a faint shadow flickered on the wall. They tiptoed around the corner to see where it was coming from. Down the hall they saw Mrs. Harrison in her office with only her desk light on.

"What's she doing?" whispered Annie so quietly Aariz could barely hear her.

"She's looking through her desk drawers," whispered Aariz.

"I bet that's where she hid the money," said Annie confidently. "She came back tonight to get it."

"We don't know that," whispered Aariz a bit too harshly.

Mrs. Harrison suddenly stopped, snapped her head toward the partly opened door, and peered out.

Just then the main lights came on and lit up the library. Annie and Aariz jumped and looked around. Miss Roberts walked in and saw Annie and Aariz staring at her with wide eyes.

"What are you two doing here?"

At the same time, Mrs. Harrison came out of her office and quickly walked over to all three of them. "What are you all doing here!?"

"I left my cell phone and came back to get it," said Miss Roberts, still confused at seeing everyone in the library after hours.

Annie and Aariz looked at each other helplessly.

"We were hoping to find the real robber," said Annie in a low voice. "It can't be Mr. Lasker. There must be a mistake."

"There certainly is!" said Mrs. Harrison angrily. "And you two made it. I'm calling your parents."

4

The next day, Annie and Aariz entered the library and slowly walked over to the main desk to return a pile of books.

"Why the long faces?" asked Miss Roberts. "Were your parents angry?"

"We're both grounded from everything except school and the library," said Aariz with a frown.

"Which isn't all that bad," said Annie. "That's where we usually spend our time anyway."

Annie leaned in closer to Miss Roberts. "We wanted to talk to you," said Annie. "Mrs. Harrison was acting suspicious last night, and *she* never told us what *she* was doing here."

"Well," said Miss Roberts, "she is the head librarian. I know she's gruff sometimes, but she's very serious when it comes to the library. She works late most days."

Mrs. Harrison saw the three of them from across the room and walked over to where they were standing. "Cathy, do you have a moment?"

Annie and Aariz excused themselves, then walked over behind a nearby bookshelf and looked back at the two librarians.

"Did you see that?" said Annie. "She doesn't want us talking to Miss Roberts."

"It's just a coincidence," replied Aariz.

"Cathy," began Mrs. Harrison, searching for the right words to explain herself. "When I was putting books away earlier, they didn't go back on the shelves where I thought they should go. Instead, I had to put them back several rows over. Strange. All the other books on the shelves seemed to be in order. And these are old reference books that are never used. Did we get books in that I'm not aware of?"

Miss Roberts laughed and waved her hand dismissively. "No, I don't think so. I think you've been working too hard, Emma."

"Or too long," added Mrs. Harrison wistfully. "I need a vacation...or even retirement."

"Did you hear that?" whispered Aariz.

"Shh!" answered Annie. "Keep listening." Annie pretended to look for a book on a shelf when one of the assistant librarians looked over at them suspiciously.

"I heard that the police searched the entire library. They looked between all the books on the shelves," continued Miss Roberts. "They especially looked in the old bank basement where they found the money. But they didn't find any more. They think Mr. Lasker hid it there, then took it out later and spent it. It was almost $2,000. They're still building a case."

"I do agree with those children about Mr. Lasker," said Mrs. Harrison. "I've known Ed Lasker for thirty years. It just doesn't fit."

"I guess you never really know people," said Miss Roberts.

5

Aariz glanced at the clock on the wall. "Annie, I think we should go home now," he said. "It's getting late, and I don't want to upset my parents further... Annie?"

Annie stared straight ahead, lost in thought. "I...I think I know where the missing money is, Aariz. And it's still in the library."

"But the police looked," said Aariz.

She led Aariz over to the reference shelves where Mrs. Harrison said she returned the books. "I know this Encyclopedia volume belongs here." Annie pointed to the first volume. "It was here last month because when I took out *Anne of Green Gables*, I looked up the book description in this encyclopedia."

Annie walked over a few shelves. "If Mrs. Harrison thought those books should have gone here instead, then something is different between this volume and where she put them back."

"But Mrs. Harrison wouldn't tell anyone if she was hiding something on these shelves," countered Aariz.

"Maybe the money is hidden between these reference books," said Annie. "We're talking about 300 books."

Again, Aariz objected. "But the police looked between all the books on the shelves and they didn't find anything..."

Suddenly, they both looked at each other with wide eyes. "They looked *between* the books..." said Annie.

"Aariz," said Annie. "We have to look *inside* these reference books."

"Already there, Annie." Aariz was opening the second volume of the encyclopedia. "Nothing here."

Annie checked the reference books further down the shelf. "Nothing here, either."

When Aariz had finished with the entire encyclopedia set, he moved over to the next shelf. "*Accounting Desk Reference 1986*. Who would look at this?" He opened the book. Nope... I hope this isn't a waste of time."

"Keep looking," urged Annie.

After twenty minutes, at book eighty-five, Aariz opened *Unusual Aztec Translations*. His eyes and mouth went wide. All the pages were cut out, replaced by dozens of dollar bills.

Annie rushed over and looked. "I knew it! I knew Mr. Lasker didn't do it. That's what Mrs. Harrison was doing that night. These are her books! I'm going to report her to Miss Roberts and the police."

6

"Slow down, Annie," said Miss Roberts. "What's this about? Mrs. Harrison has left for the day."

Annie explained to Miss Roberts what she and Aariz had found. "You've got to call the police, Miss Roberts. I'm sure she's the one who stole the money."

Miss Roberts looked around, took a deep breath, and exhaled. "Not here, where people can hear us. Stay here while I go to my office and make the call."

Aariz had stayed back among the bookshelves to make sure that no one bothered their "crime scene."

He was about to sit in a chair when he saw Mr. Lasker's cleaning gloves lying there. *I hope Mr. Lasker is all right*, thought Aariz. Strange, though—Mr. Lasker never left anything lying about. What are these gloves doing here?

A minute later, he saw Miss Roberts hurrying back to the shelves. She looked around, then quickly opened and closed several books in that section.

Aariz was puzzled. How did she know which books on the shelves to look at?

When she finished reviewing the books, she put them back and walked back over to Annie at the main desk.

"Did you call the police?" asked Annie.

Before Miss Roberts could answer, Aariz quickly walked over and interrupted them. "Come on, Annie. We don't want to get into more trouble with our parents. The library's about to close, so we'd better get going."

Annie looked doubtfully at him but said nothing. After a moment, she turned to Miss Roberts. "Well, goodnight Miss Roberts. Tomorrow will you tell us what the police said?"

"Goodnight, Annie, Aariz. I'll make sure I fill you in on what they say. There's nothing anyone will do tonight."

As the two walked to the door, Aariz looked over his shoulder and quickly pulled Annie behind a bookshelf.

"What are you doing, Aariz? I thought we were leaving. And haven't we hidden behind enough bookshelves?"

"Shh," replied Aariz. "No, we're not leaving—yet. And we may have to hide behind a few more shelves before the day is over."

7

Ten minutes later, the library lights went out. Soon everything was dark and completely still.

"Now *I'm* worried about our parents," whispered Annie. "What are we doing?"

"I don't think Miss Roberts called the police," said Aariz. "Keep your eyes on that bookshelf." Aariz pointed to the shelf where Mrs. Harrison had returned the books. "Mrs. Harrison never saw Miss Roberts actually put the money in the safe. She just assumed that she did..."

Just then, they saw a flashlight beam flicker on the other side of the library. Annie gasped. "Shouldn't we call the police?"

"Shh! Just watch," whispered Aariz. He reached for his cell phone. He was glad that his mom let him use it even though he was grounded. Quietly, Aariz started the video camera.

The flashlight beam was the only thing visible as it flashed around the darkened room. Neither Annie nor Aariz could make out who was using it. Then the beam stopped, illuminating the bookshelf where Mrs. Harrison had been the night before.

Aariz wished he had more light. So far, his video wouldn't show much. Suddenly, they heard books being removed from the shelves. The video still wasn't getting a good picture though.

He waved to Annie to back up with him, changed his phone to dial, tapped in 911, and began whispering to an operator.

As Annie moved backward, she knocked over a chair and tumbled to the floor with a crash. The flashlight swung over quickly as a voice shouted out, "Who's there!?"

Annie and Aariz ran as fast as they could out the library door. Outside, police cars with flashing lights were pulling into the library parking lot.

Stolen

8

The next day, Mrs. Harrison wasn't as grumpy as usual. She even managed a small smile when she saw Annie and Aariz enter the library. Mr. Lasker, who was now back at the library, waved to them as he pushed a cleaning cart to the Community Room.

Annie and Aariz sheepishly walked up to Mrs. Harrison. "We're sorry for all the trouble we caused," said Aariz.

Mrs. Harrison raised her eyebrows and smiled. "Why, I was going to apologize to you two," she said. "Thank you for clearing Mr. Lasker's name. And for clearing my name. I never even realized that I was a suspect."

"We thought," stammered Annie. "That you were the one... We didn't even think of Miss Roberts..."

Mrs. Harrison nodded and smiled. "Maybe if I wasn't so grumpy all the time?"

Annie and Aariz both winced.

"We can all learn from this," continued Mrs. Harrison. "I never even thought to check why those books were out of place. It's so obvious now. The police caught Miss Roberts inside the library last night with all the missing money stuffed into a grocery bag. All the books that she had hollowed out and hidden the money in were scattered on the floor.

"She only pretended to put the money in the safe that evening. She closed the safe and I never paid any attention to it. She knew Mr. Lasker had the safe combination. So, using his rubber gloves to hide her fingerprints, she put some of the money in the bank deposit box to throw suspicion at him."

"But why did she even hide the money?" asked Aariz. "Why didn't she just take it home?"

"She knew I worked late a lot, usually at the front desk. She didn't think I'd discover that the money was missing so soon. It was a lot of money to take out right in front of me all at once, so the next day she hid the money in those books while she was on break.

"The police said that she had hid money in them before. She got the idea when she was at the city library book sale last month. She bought books that she thought no one would ever look at. She hid the money in them when she thought it was too risky to remove it so soon from the library.

"She might have gotten away with it if you two didn't figure it out. How *did* you two figure it out?

"Something wasn't right about those books on the shelves," said Aariz. "There were too many new books. We knew the money wasn't between the books..."

"So then it hit us: we figured the money must be inside the books," finished Annie. "Or at least some of them—those extra books that you found."

"I see why you two do so well in school," said Mrs. Harrison.

Annie and Aariz both smiled. This was better than one of their mystery books.

"But you know, Annie," continued Mrs. Harrison with a sudden mock frown. "*Anne of Green Gables* was overdue when you returned it. You owe a fine."

Annie's face dropped. Mrs. Harrison quickly smiled. "But I think we can forgive that fee this time. And Aariz, I think there were some baked goods left over from the sale." Mrs. Harrison motioned over to the front desk. "I believe they now belong to you."

Raspberry brownie cakes and caramel filled cupcakes as a reward? Aariz could live with that.

About The Author

Bob Wonders is a designer who lives with his wife and son in Manlius, NY. He discovered Story Shares when looking for reading material to help increase his son's interest in reading. He applauds Story Shares's efforts in helping teens and young adults improve their literacy.

About The Publisher

Story Shares is a nonprofit focused on supporting the millions of teens and adults who struggle with reading by creating a new shelf in the library specifically for them. The ever-growing collection features content that is compelling and culturally relevant for teens and adults, yet still readable at a range of lower reading levels.

Story Shares generates content by engaging deeply with writers, bringing together a community to create this new kind of book. With more intriguing and approachable stories to choose from, the teens and adults who have fallen behind are improving their skills and beginning to discover the joy of reading. For more information, visit storyshares.org.

Easy to Read. Hard to Put Down.

Stolen

www.ingramcontent.com/pod-product-compliance
Lightning Source LLC
Chambersburg PA
CBHW071229170626
46809CB00005BA/1984

* 9 7 8 1 6 4 2 6 1 5 3 9 5 *